EGMONT

We bring stories to life

First published in Great Britain in 2006
by Egmont UK Limited
239 Kensington High Street, London W8 6SA
Illustrated by Niall Harding
Postman Pat © 2006 Woodland Animations Ltd,
a division of Entertainment Rights PLC.
Licensed by Entertainment Rights PLC.
Original writer John Cunliffe.
From the original television design by Ivor Wood
Royal Mail and Post Office imagery is used by kind
permission of Royal Mail Group plc.
All rights reserved.

ISBN 978 1 4052 2410 9
ISBN 1 4052 2410 X
1 2 3 4 5 6 7 8 9 10
Printed in Singapore

Postman Pat's
Big Book of Words

sun

hot air
balloon

mountain

van

police
car

trees

post office

church

Pat's house

road

stone wall

train station

grass

GREENDALE

footbridge

railway line

platform

Postman Pat's House

sun

bird

chimney

roof

door

rabbit

gate

Sara

cupboard

fridge

bread

sink

oven

table

chair

plate

fish bone

Jess

poster · Julian · curtains · clock · bed · drawer · books · ball

shampoo · mirror · window · taps · towel · Pat · bath

picture · vase · chair · telephone · wool · rug

On the River

willow tree

oar

rowing boat

fishing rod

river bank

Rev. Timms

Tea

canal boat

deck

net

swan

otter

reeds

plane

mast

waterfall

ship's
wheel

Jeff

cabin

life-jacket

rope

Charlie

porthole

boat

anchor

duck

paddle

canoe

fish

calendar

list

glasses

scales

bell

shawl

teapot

scissors

envelope

sack

window

door

post box

parcels

van

bicycle

flowers

tea tray

PAT 1

Post Office

Royal Mail

The Village Fête

balloon

bunting

string

cap

rope

ball

coconut

trumpet

bow

stick

drum

peg

paintbrush

Lucy

milk

paint

marquee

Dorothy

fortune teller

Julia

jelly

raffle ticket

satchel

whiskers

jam

cheese

butterfly

On the Farm

cow

apron

basket

pitchfork

churn

parcel

PAT 1

pig pen

piglets

pig

hen

School Time

kite

classroom window

football

bench

bell

teacher

playground

hopscotch

stone

jumper

flask

sandwich

school bag

flower

chart

blackboard

fox

painting

bin

plant

books

chalk

pencils

world map

coat pegs

cupboard

coats

paper

pens

desk

water mill

water wheel

van

dungarees

shovel

woolly hat

ice

scarf

gloves

boots

collar

snowman

On Holiday

Egypt

baseball cap

hat

pyramid

camel

Sphinx

shirt

guidebook

sand

coconut

sunglasses

ice-cream

bucket and spade

Australia

sea

flag

sandcastle

India

Taj Mahal

sari

America

clown

roller-coaster

bow-tie

tent

camera

The Birthday Party

green balloon

biscuits

bouncy castle

tail

cake

jelly

sandwiches

fruit

table cloth

paws

shoes

trainers

flowers

blue balloon

yellow balloon

red balloon

hat

window frame

drink

buns

present

ribbon